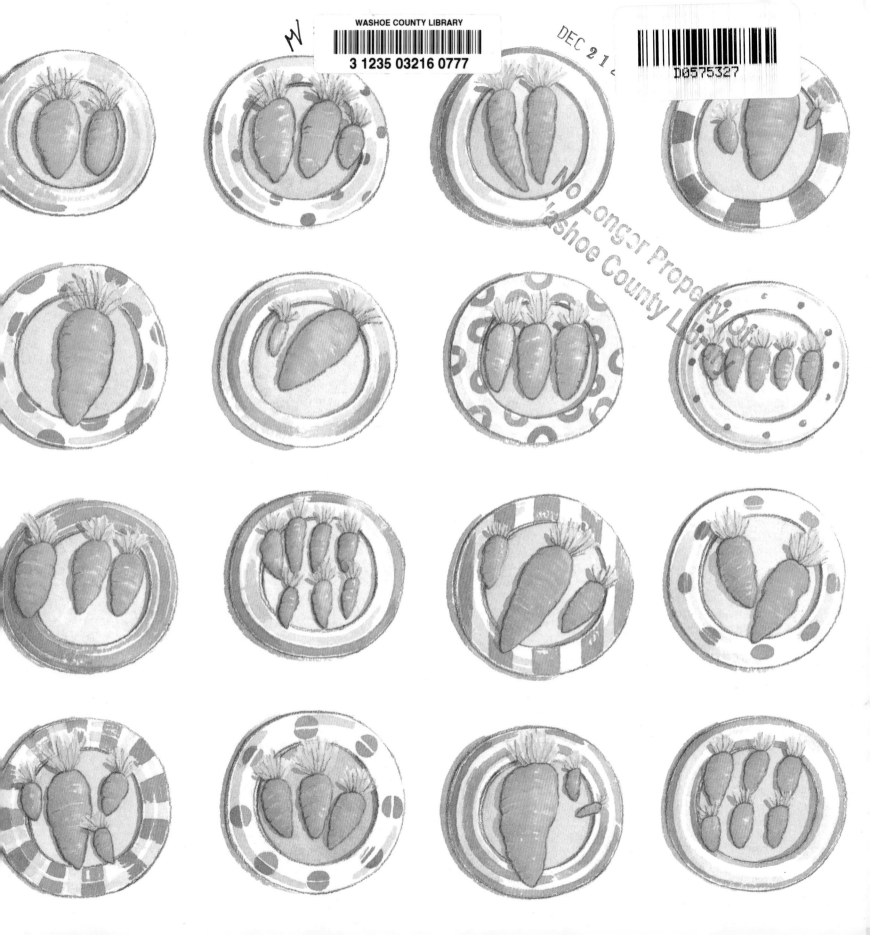

For
Aaron
and Zoë

LIBRARY OF CONGRESS CATALOGING-IN-PUBLICATION DATA
Ives, Penny.
Rabbit pie / written and illustrated by Penny Ives.
p. cm.
Summary: Mama Rabbit has a recipe for tending to her six little ones
and getting them ready for bed.
ISBN 0-670-05951-X (hardcover)
[1. Rabbits—Fiction. 2. Bedtime—Fiction.] I. Title.
PZ7.I1949Rab 2006
[E]—dc22
2005008071

VIKING
Published by Penguin Group
Penguin Young Readers Group,
345 Hudson Street, New York,
New York 10014, U.S.A.

Penguin Books Ltd, Registered
Offices: 80 Strand, London
WC2R 0RL, England

First published in the U.S.A.
in 2006 by Viking,
a division of Penguin Young
Readers Group

Published simultaneously in
Great Britain in Puffin Books

1 3 5 7 9 10 8 6 4 2

Rabbit Pie

By PENNY IVES

VIKING

First gather together your ingredients.

1 game of hide-and-seek

1 bath

6 pairs of pajamas

6 cups of milk

1 story

A sprinkling of soft kisses

6 large carrots

Then . . .

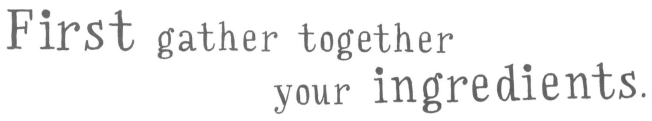

...find
six
small
rabbits...

...if
you
can!

Take off any
dirty
bits and . . .

... place in warm **soapy** water.

Gently scrub.

Watch **very** closely.

Fold
into a
soft
towel

and allow to **cool** down.

Pat dry,
dust
the bottoms...

and **lightly**
brush
the tops.

Slowly pour in

six
cups
of milk.

Tuck in,
sprinkling
with
kisses.

Leave in a **warm** place until morning.

When
quite ready,
serve with
fresh
carrots.

Sweet
Rabbit
Pie!

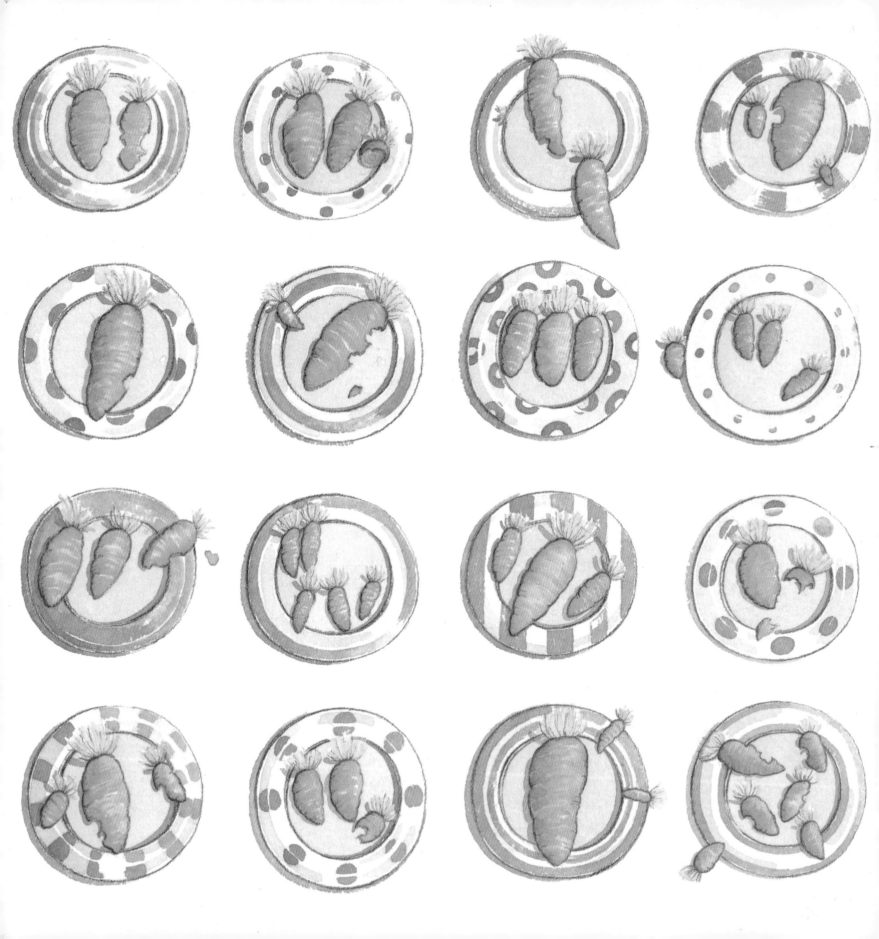